The Lady who was Beautiful Inside

for Victoria

HarperCollins*Entertainment*
An Imprint of HarperCollins*Publishers*
77–85 Fulham Palace Road,
Hammersmith, London W6 8JB

www.harpercollins.co.uk

Published by HarperCollins*Entertainment* 2004
3 5 7 9 8 6 4

A catalogue record for this book
is available from the British Library

ISBN 0 00 717799 2

Printed and bound by Proost

The LADY who was BEAUTIFUL INSIDE

There was once
a LADY.

One day when she was sitting at the HAIRDRESSER She picked up a magazine.

"Oh, hairdresser," she said. "Look at all these BEAUTIFUL ladies. See how their LEGS reach up to the sky. See how their BOSOMS are firm and perfect.

" See how every GLOSSY hair lies perfectly in place. And see how they have no sign of CROW'S-FEET EYES or ORANGE-PEEL BOTTOM.

"Why do I BOTHER, hairdresser? Why? Why? WHY?"

And she held the leg of the hairdresser and began to SOB noiselessly into his trousers.

"Lady," said the hairdresser, "do not DESPAIR. Look at your SMILE."

The lady LOOKED.

"Nobody has a smile as BEAUTIFUL as you," said the hairdresser. Not even the ladies in the magazines. And that, lady, is because your beauty comes from DEEP WITHIN you. And that is the most beautiful BEAUTY of all."

"Oh, hairdresser," said the lady, "do you think so? Do you REALLY think so?"

"I KNOW so," said the hairdresser. "Just take a walk outside and you will see."

At that, the hairdresser
VANISHED and the lady
walked out of the salon
into the rain.

As she SMILED, an amazing thing happened. The rain stopped and the SUN broke through the clouds.

Flowers BLOOMED in her footsteps, birds began to SING and the trees burst into BLOSSOM.

The people in the street began to CHEER and little children DANCED all around her in a circle, LAUGHING.

"Well I never!" exclaimed the lady, a little flustered. "Oh goodness gracious me!

"Could it be that the hairdresser was RIGHT or is this just a STRANGE and FORTUNATE coincidence?"

In the end it did not matter.
For the lady had seen the
POWER of the beauty
INSIDE her.

And from then on, everywhere
she went, LOVELINESS
happened.

For she did have a
very BEAUTIFUL
beauty indeed.

THE END